Marketplace Leadership Workbook

Spiritual Tools for Today's Successful Leaders

Dale Jones

Heritage Publishing

Marketplace Leadership Workbook:
Spiritual Tools for Today's Successful Leaders
Copyright ©2024 by Dale Jones

9 8 7 6 5 4 3 2 1

PRINTED IN THE UNITED STATES OF AMERICA
Heritage Publishing

ISBN 979821859034-5

Table of Contents

CHAPTER 1

CHRIST IN THE MARKETPLACE

One of the greatest desires of pastors is to see their parishioners engaged in bringing Christ into the marketplace and making disciples of men. The term *marketplace* refers to places where people gather outside the four walls of the church. The marketplace is the ideal setting for believers to be witnesses of God's grace and love to unbelievers because it encompasses all the places you spend your time, whether you're going to school, shopping, working, taking a vacation, walking in your neighborhood, or enjoying a concert.

The activities and reflection questions in this chapter will help you to look outside your church sanctuary to minister and align with God's assignment of making disciples where people are. Jesus said, "The harvest is plentiful, but the laborers are few. Pray earnestly to the Lord of the harvest to send out laborers into the harvest."

Define Your Marketplace

Where is your marketplace? Think of all the places you go to regularly. Then create a marketplace map. In the space below, draw and label shapes (for example, circles, squares, or triangles) to represent where you spend the most time (not including church): home, work, gym, school, park, etc. Everyone's map will look different depending on the places you go. Under your map, list the people you might engage in ministry in each place.

Reflect

1. Where do you spend time when you're not at church?

2. How can you bring God into these places?

3. If you are already ministering in the marketplace, how have you seen God at work there?

4. If you are not ministering in the marketplace, what is holding you back? Why?

5. What can you do to move forward with marketplace ministry?

Be Salt and Light

In the Sermon on the Mount, Jesus taught believers to be the salt of the earth and the light of the world. This means we should reflect Christ, add value wherever we go, and illuminate dark places. And by saying "the earth" or "the world," Jesus gave us permission to step outside the sanctuary and minister to a broader swath of people all around us.

When you enter the marketplace this week, be intentional about engaging people differently. Do one thing that reflects being "salt" (bringing out goodness) and one thing that reflects being "light" (bringing clarity or truth). Record your experiences below.

Day 1
Salt action:

Light action:

Day 2
Salt action:

Light action:

Reflect

1. When you engaged as "salt" and "light" this week, what were people's reactions?

2. During your interactions, were you courageous or fearful? Why?

3. What did you learn during your "salt and light" ministry?

4. What is your strategy for bringing out goodness and reflecting clarity and truth for the future?

Challenges in the Marketplace

Everyone will not respond positively to your ministry in the marketplace. You may face skepticism, resistance, or even hostility. However, Jesus tells us to be wise but harmless when we engage with others.

Scenario

Read the following scenario, and answer the questions below: Someone challenges your faith in a public setting.

1. As a representative of Jesus Christ, how would you react?

2. What key points could you make to engage in a meaningful discussion rather than an argument?

Role-Play

With a partner or in a small group, role-play a challenging scenario that could happen in the marketplace. Invite one or two people to act as skeptics, while one shows how to respond with wisdom and grace. Switch roles. As a group, discuss how the role-play went. In the space below, reflect on what you learned from both sides of the role-play.

Overcoming Our Fears of Sharing Christ in the Marketplace

Often, we avoid witnessing for Christ because we are afraid of what people might do or think about us. Our fear is rooted in our concern that people might reject us, laugh at us, or ignore us. But when we trust God that He has made every provision for us and has equipped and empowered us to witness for Him, we can confidently fulfill our assignment. When we approach others with love, humility, and respect, we reflect Christ's character and open doors for sharing His love.

Reflect

1. What fears do you experience when sharing your faith in the marketplace, and how have these fears affected your willingness to engage with others?

2. If you already share Christ with people in your marketplace, what gives you the courage to exercise faith over fear?

Role-Play

In a small group or with a partner, act out a scenario where fear might arise as you interact with a person (for example, a colleague who challenges your beliefs, or you're hesitant to start a faith-based conversation). Invite one group member to play the role of the fearful person, while the other offers encouragement and practical strategies for overcoming fear. Switch roles and discuss what you learned. Use the space below to journal a few notes on how you can overcome any fears you have about sharing Christ in the marketplace.

Engage With Purpose

Purposeful engagement in the marketplace requires intentionality. This means going beyond casual interactions to seek opportunities to share Christ through what you say and do.

Planning for Purpose

Think about people you feel called to engage with. Write down a plan for the next week that includes the following:

- Build relationships by showing genuine interest in others' lives.
- Find ways to serve your coworkers, neighbors, and friends.
- Share your personal testimony or faith-based insight when the opportunity arises.
- Plan to follow up and keep building those relationships.

Innovation in Marketplace Ministry

Use creative and contemporary methods to reach people where they are, especially in today's digital age. Then consider the following:

- How can you integrate your faith into your online presence in a nonintrusive way?

- Brainstorm creative ideas for bringing a message of hope to your online networks (for example, blog posts, short inspirational videos, and Bible verses).

Technology and Ministry

Choose one digital platform (social media, email, blog, or website), and develop a plan to share one message of faith this week. In the space below, describe the content you will share and why you believe it will resonate with your followers.

Promote Christ Through Ethical Practices

Part of being Christ's witness in the marketplace is living out your faith through ethical and fair practices.

Case Study

Read the following case study, and answer the questions below: You have a prestigious position at a high-profile company. Your team leader tells you to exaggerate product benefits to close deals. You feel conflicted because your faith calls you to be honest.

1. How should you handle this situation?

2. What could be a God-honoring way to balance your job's demands with your ethical standards?

3. Think of a situation in your marketplace where you've faced a similar ethical dilemma. How did you handle it?

4. In retrospect, what would you do differently to reflect Christ more clearly?

Going Outside Your Comfort Zone

God often calls us to step beyond our comfort zones to reach people in unexpected places. Jesus spent a lot of time ministering outside traditional religious settings.

Reflect

1. What areas of ministry have you been avoiding? Why?

2. What would it take for you to move forward in these areas?

Next Steps

- This week, pray for the people in your marketplace. Ask God for wisdom, courage, and opportunities to share His love. Make a prayer list for people you feel called to engage with, and commit to praying for them daily.
- Revisit your marketplace map, and plan to expand it. Identify one new place or group of people where you could minister. Pray for God to open doors for meaningful connections.

Prayer

Lord, help me to look around my marketplace and see opportunities to represent You there. Give me the courage, wisdom, and discernment to engage with and serve those I meet. Amen.

CHAPTER 2

THE INTERSECTION OF WORK AND FAITH

Integrating your faith into your work and daily life can be challenging. However, Jesus modeled the proper work/life balance through His ministry in the marketplace, His relationship with His disciples, and His need to withdraw for time alone.

In this chapter, you will learn how to balance your professional life with your calling to be a light in the world.

Jesus in the Marketplace

Jesus made 92 percent of His public appearances in the marketplace. He didn't wait for people to come to Him; He went where the people were. This strategy shows the importance of meeting people in their everyday environments.

Case Study

Consider the following scenario: A coworker confides in you about his struggle to keep up with his high-stress position while keeping his family together. You recognize an opportunity to offer support and share Christ's love, but you aren't sure what you should say to him without overstepping professional boundaries.

1. What do you think Jesus would do in this situation?

2. How can you offer support while remaining professional?

3. What mistakes have you made in having a proper work/life balance?

4. What successes have you had?

Role-Play

With a partner, role-play the coworker scenario. Then switch roles and show how you might have a compassionate conversation with the coworker, offering support without being intrusive or unprofessional. Discuss what you learned.

Marketplace Leadership

God equips His people through diverse giftings within the church such as apostles, prophets, evangelists, pastors, and teachers to prepare us for marketplace ministry. The equipping of the saints makes us more able in our everyday lives to make a difference wherever we go.

Reflect

1. How have you been equipped to serve more effectively in the marketplace?

2. How can you use your gifts to influence and serve others?

3. Think of a time when your gift(s) helped someone. What was the impact?

4. If you're unsure of your God-given gift(s) or how to apply it to your ministry, list steps you can take to seek direction.

Developing Discernment

Effective ministry requires discernment. We need to know when to speak up and when to let our actions speak for us. Balancing work responsibilities with a Christian witness is essential to maintain credibility and influence.

Reflect

1. When have you used discernment at work? What was the outcome?

2. Write down examples of areas where you could improve.

Building Relationships in the Marketplace

Jesus built relationships with a wide range of people. By forming genuine connections, we create opportunities to share God's love naturally and effectively.

Relationship Building Plan

Study the two examples below. Then list three people you feel called to build a deeper relationship with in your marketplace. For each person, write one practical step you will take this week to strengthen your connection. Later, if there is a measurable outcome, record that, too.

Examples

Person: *Jessica (coworker)*
Step: *Invite her to lunch, and ask how she's been handling her work/life balance.*
Outcome: *Jessica has asked you to be her mentor. Check in with her, and offer feedback as appropriate.*

Person: *Lawrence (manager at your bank)*
Step: *A few weeks ago, he mentioned his wife's illness. Follow up by asking him how he and his family are doing, and offer to continue to pray for them.*
Outcome: *Things are looking up, but Lawrence's wife has a long journey ahead in her recovery. He appreciates your encouragement and prayers. Look for ways to continue to show God's love to Lawrence in the months ahead.*

Overcoming the Fear of Balancing Our Work and Faith

Some believers struggle with figuring out how to combine their work and faith. Achieving that delicate balance can seem like an overwhelming task. But God calls us to balance professionalism with a bold yet respectful witness for Christ and a commitment to live out our beliefs authentically. By relying on God's wisdom and seeking opportunities to lead with integrity, we can bridge the gap between faith and work.

The Holy Spirit empowers us to overcome challenges and confidently reflect God's love in any professional setting. You can reflect Christ's character without compromising workplace standards. Trusting God to guide your actions and conversations helps turn fear into opportunities for meaningful impact.

Reflect

1. In what areas of your work do you feel the most tension between your faith and professional responsibilities? How can you trust God's wisdom to navigate these challenges?

2. How do you currently demonstrate integrity in your work? How can you improve to more authentically reflect Christ's character in your workplace?

Innovation in Ministry

To reach the marketplace effectively, we must be innovative and adaptable. Jesus used parables, healing, and direct conversations to reach people. Today, we can use technology, creativity, and new approaches to bring the gospel to others.

Creative Ministry Plan

Think of one new way to share your faith at work or in your community. This could be as simple as starting a lunchtime discussion group or creating inspirational content for social media.

1. Idea

2. Target Audience

3. First Step

Ethics and Integrity

Our actions should reflect Christ's characteristics and our integrity. Our character should shine through in business dealings, leadership, or interpersonal interactions.

Case Study

Consider the following scenario: You notice a culture of cutting corners at your workplace, but you're hesitant to speak out for fear of being ostracized. As a Christian, how should you approach this situation?

Reflect

1. What characteristics have you seen successfully reflected in the marketplace?

2. What characteristics do you struggle to show?

3. How can you develop integrity and grow as a marketplace leader?

4. How can you more closely align your work with biblical values?

Leading Like Jesus

Jesus led with compassion, humility, and wisdom. As marketplace leaders, we are called to emulate these qualities and lead by example.

Leadership Assessment

1. Evaluate your leadership style. How well do you reflect Jesus' leadership qualities in your work?

2. List three areas where you can grow as a Christ-like leader.

Living Out Your Faith

Remember that every moment in the marketplace is an opportunity to reflect Christ. You can make a significant impact through small acts of kindness, ethical decision-making, or intentional relationships.

Reflect

Write a short prayer asking God to help you live out your faith boldly. Commit to pursuing excellence, integrity, and compassion in all that you do.

Next Steps

- This week, practice discernment in your workplace by observing when to speak about your faith and when to let your actions speak for you. Reflect on where your approach helped strengthen your witness.
- Identify one Christ-like leadership characteristic—humility, compassion, or integrity—that you'd like to improve. Apply this characteristic to your interactions in your marketplace. Then reflect on how this change affected your relationships and effectiveness as a leader.

Prayer

Lord, help me to see every moment as a chance to live a life of integrity. Guide my actions, words, and decisions so that I may lead effectively and ethically, reflect Your kingdom, and draw others closer to You. Amen.

CHAPTER 3

CREATION THEOLOGY

Creation theology is foundational to our faith, emphasizing that we are created in God's image and responsible for representing Him in the world. Understanding our role in creation allows us to live with purpose and engage with the world as God's representatives.

In this chapter, you will explore the intersection of faith and work through creation theology, emphasizing the importance of reflecting God's image in the marketplace. You will understand God's purpose for you as His image-bearer and representative.

God's Design

Reflect

1. How does knowing that you are made in God's image affect your view of yourself and others?

2. How does creation theology challenge or confirm your understanding of God's purpose for humanity?

God's Image

Study the example below. Then write down three of God's characteristics that He shares with humanity (for example, love, wisdom, and creativity). Think about how you can display these traits in your daily interactions at work and in your community.

<u>Example</u>
Characteristic: *Creativity*
Application: *Use creativity to solve problems at work, taking on challenges with an open mind and a positive attitude.*

God as Creator and Worker

During creation, God worked for six days and rested on the seventh, establishing a pattern of work and rest for mankind.

Reflect

1. How does your work reflect God's creativity and purpose?

2. In what ways can you honor God through your work, regardless of your profession?

Work as Worship

This week, approach your work as an act of worship. At the end of each day, write a brief reflection on how this mindset affected your attitude, performance, and interactions with others.

Humanity as Co-Creators

As image-bearers of God, we are called to be co-creators with Him. This means taking care of the earth and using what God has given us in ways that please Him.

Stewardship in the Marketplace

Identify one area where you can practice better stewardship (for example, managing resources wisely or helping others grow in their potential). Write down three specific actions to improve stewardship in that area.

The Fall and Its Impact

The Fall disrupted humanity's perfect relationship with God but did not destroy our purpose. Through Christ, we are restored to our role as God's representatives.

Reflect

1. How does the reality of sin and brokenness affect your view of work and relationships?

2. In what ways can you live out the restored image of God in a broken world?

Restoring God's Image

Think of one relationship or situation at work where brokenness is evident. Write a plan to restore this situation by reflecting Christ's love, wisdom, and grace.

Overcoming the Fear of Being God's Representative

Creation theology helps us recognize that we are created in God's image and called to represent Him in every aspect of our lives, including our work. By embracing our role as co-creators with God, we can confidently engage in the marketplace, turning everyday actions into opportunities to reflect God's original design for us and His creation.

Reflect

1. What worries you about being God's representative in the marketplace? How does recognizing that you are made in God's image influence how you approach your role in the workplace?

2. In what ways can viewing yourself as a co-creator with God empower you to overcome fear and boldly represent Him in your daily work?

Reflection Chart

Distribute a piece of paper and a pencil or pen to each group member. Ask group members to make two columns, one titled "God's Image in Me" and the other "My Work." In the first column, list characteristics of God that you reflect (for example, creativity, wisdom, compassion). In the second column, write down ways you can demonstrate these attributes in your work. In the space below, reflect on any areas where you feel challenged and make a plan to grow in those areas.

Divine Resemblance

We are called to resemble God in public and in private. The marketplace is an ideal arena where we can reflect God's image.

Reflect

1. In what ways do your actions and decisions reflect God's character?

2. How can you improve your witness?

Demonstrating God's Character

Read through the list below of God's characteristics that He shares with us. Each day next week, choose one of the characteristics to demonstrate in your workplace or community. Then write down the ways you lived out that characteristic.

<u>The Characteristics God Shares With Humanity</u>

resourcefulness	wisdom	holiness	faithfulness
creativity	mercy	patience	justice
righteousness	wrath	grace	love
goodness	truthfulness	kindness	jealousy

Characteristic:
How I lived it out:

Characteristic:
How I lived it out:

Characteristic:
How I lived it out:

Characteristic:
How I lived it out:

Characteristic:
How I lived it out:

Characteristic:
How I lived it out:

Characteristic:
How I lived it out:

Aligning With God's Purpose

Reflect

1. What specific "good works" has God prepared you to do in your marketplace?

2. How can you align your work with God's greater purpose for your life?

Purpose-Driven Work

Set a purpose-driven goal for this month. Consider how your role can contribute to something bigger than yourself, whether serving others, solving problems, improving processes, or helping your team succeed. Track your progress.

God's Representatives

The marketplace is a challenging place where we face opposition and ethical dilemmas. It is important to learn how to navigate these challenges using wisdom and discernment.

Reflect

1. What challenges do you face in reflecting Christ in your workplace or community?

2. How can you overcome these challenges in ways that honor God?

Scenario

Read the following scenario: Imagine you are facing an ethical dilemma at work where honesty could cost you a promotion. Write down how you would respond, considering your role as God's representative.

A Marketplace Mindset

Your work is not separate from your ministry. Cultivate a mindset where your job becomes a mission field where you can influence others for Christ.

Reflect

1. How can you view your work as an opportunity for ministry?

2. What steps can you take to make your faith more visible in your professional life without compromising your commitment to your work?

Ministry Action Plan

Write a ministry action plan for your workplace. This can include goals such as building relationships, offering prayer support, or starting a Bible study group. Set specific, measurable steps to achieve these goals.

Living Out Creation Theology

Reflect

1. How can you integrate God's original design for you into your daily life and work?

2. What habits can you develop to remind yourself of your role as God's representative?

Daily Habit Tracker

Create a daily habit tracker to ensure that you are living out your assignment as God's representative. Track habits such as daily prayer, acts of kindness, integrity in decisions, and opportunities to share your faith.

Embracing Your Role as God's Representative

Remember that God has placed you in the marketplace for a reason. You are His image-bearer called to reflect His love, wisdom, and creativity in all you do.

Prayer Exercise

Write a prayer asking God to help you fully embrace your role as His representative in the marketplace. Commit to living out your faith boldly and consistently in every area of your life.

Next Steps

- Set a monthly goal for how you will live out your role as God's representative in your work.
- Continue to reflect on creation theology in your personal and professional life, seeking to grow in your understanding of God's purpose for you.

Prayer

Lord, help me to see my work as a way of worshiping You. Create in me a spirit of excellence so I will represent You in a manner that will please You and point others to You. Amen.

CHAPTER 4
RESTORATION OF THE IMAGE OF GOD

God's original design for mankind involves work, dominion, and stewardship. We were created to live in perfect harmony with God, one another, and the natural world. But the Fall was a detour from God's plan, leading to a broken world of sin, fear, and confusion.

In this chapter, you will explore the importance of being restored to the image of God and how that applies to leadership, service, and daily life. You will also learn how to align your actions with God's original design.

Restoration of God's Image
God created humanity in His image to work, have dominion, and steward creation, but the Fall disrupted this design. Through Jesus Christ, God's plan for restoring us to His original design is in motion. Understanding this restoration allows us to live out our divine purpose in the world, especially as we serve and lead in the marketplace.

Understanding the Fall and Restoration
The fall of mankind introduced fear and a misunderstanding of purpose, but God's plan for redemption through Christ restores us to His image.

Reflect
1. How does the Fall affect your understanding of your identity and purpose?

2. What does it mean for you to be restored to the image of God?

Reflection on Restoration
Write down three areas of your life where you feel disconnected from God's original design. Next, describe practical steps you can take to realign with His image.

The Role of Work in God's Original Design
Work is an essential part of God's original design for us. God gave us dominion over the earth, calling us to be stewards and co-creators with Him.

Reflect
1. In what ways does your work reflect God's command to "till the ground" and be a steward of creation?

2. How does your attitude toward work align with God's original design for mankind?

Work as Worship
For one week, approach your work as an act of worship. At the end of each day, write a brief reflection on how this mindset changed your attitude, performance, and interactions with others.

Servant Leadership

Jesus modeled servant leadership by washing His disciples' feet, demonstrating that leadership is about humility and service.

Reflect

1. How can you incorporate servant leadership into your interactions at work or in your community?

2. What are the specific ways you can serve others through your leadership?

Servant Leadership in Action

Choose one person to serve this week. Write down what you did and how it affected your relationship.

Exercising Dominion and Stewardship

Exercising dominion is not about control but about stewardship. We are called to care for the resources and people around us with integrity and purpose.

Reflect

1. How do you see yourself as a steward in your workplace or community?

2. What resources or responsibilities has God entrusted to you that require careful stewardship?

Stewardship Evaluation

List three areas of your life where you have been given dominion (managing a team, caring for a family, or overseeing a project). Write down one step you will take in each area to practice better stewardship.

Aligning With God's Will in the Marketplace

As vice-regents of God, we are called to bring the kingdom of heaven to earth through our actions in the marketplace. This requires us to align our goals with God's heavenly mandates.

Reflect

1. What does it mean for you to bring "heaven to earth" in your workplace?

2. How can you align your personal and professional goals with God's purposes?

Kingdom Mindset in the Marketplace

Choose one goal you have in your work or community. Write down how achieving this goal can contribute to God's kingdom on earth. Plan to work toward this goal while keeping a kingdom mindset.

Authentic Leadership and Influence

Leadership is about influence. God has called us to use our influence to benefit others, not to dominate or control them.

Reflect

1. How do you use your influence in your current role (as a leader, coworker, parent)?

2. How can you use your influence to uplift those around you?

Influence Assessment

Identify three people you regularly interact with who are influenced by your actions or decisions. Write down one way you can affect each of them this week through encouragement, guidance, or support.

Overcoming Fear and Dysfunction

The Fall introduced fear and dysfunction, but through Christ, we are empowered to overcome these obstacles and live out our purpose.

Reflect

1. What fears or dysfunctions hold you back from fully embracing your identity as God's image-bearer?

2. How can you rely on God's power to overcome these challenges?

Facing Fear With Faith

Identify one fear or dysfunction that has been limiting you. Find a Bible verse that addresses this fear and commit to meditating on it daily. Write down how applying God's Word helps you face this fear with faith.

The Call to Productivity

God's original mandate for humanity is to be productive, not just in terms of physical work but also in bearing spiritual fruit through our lives.

Reflect

1. How can you increase your productivity in a way that aligns with God's purposes?

2. What "fruit" are you producing in your work, relationships, and community?

Fruitfulness Plan

Write down three areas where you would like to be more productive. Next to each area, list one practical thing you can do to bear more fruit in that area.

Avoiding Legalism and Embracing Grace

As we work toward restoring God's image in ourselves and others, it is important to avoid falling into legalism. Grace empowers us to serve and lead authentically.

Reflect

1. Are there areas of your life where you are operating from a place of legalism rather than grace?

2. How can you shift your mindset to embrace the grace of God in your leadership and service?

Grace vs. Legalism

Think of a situation where you have been hard on yourself or others, expecting perfection. Write down how you can approach this situation with more grace, allowing room for mistakes and growth.

Living as God's Vice-Regents

We are called to be God's vice-regents on earth, representing His authority and love. This role requires us to live out our faith in practical ways.

Reflect

1. What does it mean for you to be God's representative in your current role or position?

2. How can you better reflect God's love, justice, and righteousness in your leadership or work?

Embracing the Restoration of God's Image

God's plan to restore His image in us is at the heart of our calling. As we embrace this restoration, we can lead, serve, and work in ways that reflect His love and authority. By aligning our lives with His original design, we can make a meaningful impact in the marketplace and beyond.

Reflect

Write a prayer asking God to help you fully embrace your role as His image-bearer and vice-regent in the world. Commit to living out His purposes in all areas of your life, trusting in His grace to guide and empower you.

Next Steps

- Set specific goals for how you will live out God's image in your work and daily life.
- Continue reflecting on the themes of servant leadership, stewardship, and productivity as you grow in your faith and influence.

Prayer

Lord, restore Your image in me, and help me to reflect You in all that I do. Guide me as I lead, serve, and work for Your kingdom, bringing heaven to earth through my actions. Amen.

CHAPTER 5

GOD'S PLAN FOR WORK

Work is often viewed as oppressive, an unavoidable necessity, but a closer study of the Bible reveals a deeper and more noble understanding of work as a form of worship and service to God. From the beginning, God's plan for mankind involved meaningful and co-creative work, allowing mankind to manifest God's glory on earth.

This chapter is designed to help you explore and embrace the theological perspective on work, aligning it with God's original design. You will gain a deeper understanding of the divine purpose of work, moving beyond mere survival to meaningful service and worship.

Reclaiming the Purpose of Work

God created work as a noble endeavor, a form of worship, and a way to reflect His glory on earth. Our challenge today is to rediscover God's original design for work. Work is not just a way to make a living; it is a way to serve God, fulfill our purpose, and co-create with Him.

Understanding God's Original Design for Work

Work, as described in Genesis, was designed to be fulfilling and life-giving. It was meant to reflect God's creative nature and allow humans to participate in His plans for the world.

Reflect

1. How does the biblical understanding of work differ from modern views of work?

2. What does it mean to be a co-creator with God in your work?

The Impact of the Fall on Work

The Fall introduced hardship and toil into our experience of work, turning it into something burdensome. Yet, through Christ, we can restore the nobility of work by viewing it as a form of worship and obedience to God.

Restoration Reflection

Identify one task at work that feels particularly burdensome or tedious. Write a prayer asking God to help you see this task as an opportunity for worship and service. Reflect at the end of the week on how this shift in mindset affected your approach to the task.

Self-Actualization vs. Self-Preservation

Many people work from a place of self-preservation, driven by fear and the need to survive. God calls us to seek our purpose (self-actualization) first, trusting Him to provide for our needs.

Reflect

1. What drives your current approach to work—self-actualization or self-preservation? Why?

2. How can you refocus your work to align with God's purpose for your life?

Purpose vs. Survival

List three reasons you go to work every day. Circle the ones that reflect self-preservation. Then create a plan for how you can refocus at least one of these reasons to align with self-actualization and God's kingdom purposes.

Jesus and the Nobility of Work

Jesus modeled a life of purposeful work that was dedicated to God. He worked with excellence and compassion, serving those around Him. His example calls us to elevate our work beyond mere tasks to acts of love and service.

Reflect

1. How does Jesus' approach to work challenge your current view of your work?

2. How can you bring excellence and service into your workplace in a Christ-like manner?

Christ-like Work

For the next week, choose one area of your work to approach with the mindset of serving others as Christ did. Whether it's helping a coworker or completing a task with excellence, write down the results of this intentional effort each day.

Moving From Job to Vocation

Your job is what you are trained to do, but your work—your vocation—is what you are called to do by God. Understanding this distinction helps you pursue meaningful, purpose-driven work.

Reflect

1. Are you currently working in a job or a vocation? How can you tell?

2. How can you begin moving from a job mindset to a vocation mindset?

Job vs. Vocation Worksheet

Write down your current job title, and list the tasks you perform. Next to each task, write how it aligns (or doesn't align) with God's calling on your life. Look for ways to transform even mundane tasks into part of your vocation by serving God through them.

Overcoming Fear in the Workplace

Fear often keeps us from pursuing God's purpose in our work. We fear failure, rejection, or loss. However, faith in God's provision frees us to pursue meaningful work with confidence.

Reflect

1. What fears are holding you back from fully embracing your purpose in the workplace?

2. How can faith in God's provision help you overcome these fears?

Fear and Faith Journal

For one week, journal about a fear you face in your work. Each day, write down a Scripture or a prayer that encourages you to overcome this fear. At the end of the week, reflect on how focusing on faith has helped you address your fear.

Trusting God's Provision in Your Work

God promises to provide for our needs, allowing us to focus on our purpose and work without anxiety. Trusting in this promise frees us from the fear-driven mindset of self-preservation.

Reflect

1. In what areas of your work life do you struggle to trust God's provision?

2. How can you demonstrate trust in God's promises through your actions at work?

Trust in Action

Identify one practical step you can take this week to demonstrate your trust in God's provision. Write down the results of this step and reflect on how it influenced your faith.

Embracing Work as Worship

Work is a form of worship when it is done with the right heart and intention. When we approach our tasks with reverence for God, we elevate our labor to an act of service and devotion.

Work as Worship Challenge

For the next five days, choose one task at work that you will intentionally treat as an act of worship. Before starting the task, pray and dedicate it to God. Write down how this mindset changes your approach to the task and its outcome.

Aligning Your Work With God's Kingdom

God's kingdom is advanced when we align our work with His purposes. By bringing heaven's values into our work, we can transform our workplaces into places of justice, love, and integrity.

Reflect

1. How can your work contribute to God's kingdom on earth?

2. In what ways can you bring kingdom values into your workplace?

Kingdom Impact Plan

Write down three kingdom values you want to emphasize in your work. For each value, list one specific action you will take this week to demonstrate that value in your workplace.

Living as God's Co-Creator

God invites us to be co-creators with Him, using our gifts and talents to shape the world around us. By embracing this role, we participate in God's ongoing work of creation and restoration.

Reflect

1. How can you use your unique gifts to co-create with God in your workplace or community?

2. What specific project or initiative can you start to bring God's creative power into your environment?

Co-Creator Project

Choose one project or initiative in your workplace or community where you can use your gifts to co-create with God. Write a plan for how you will start this project, including specific steps, resources needed, and the impact you hope it will have.

Reclaiming the Nobility of Work

Work is more than a job. It is a divine calling that allows us to serve, worship, and co-create with God. As you align your work with God's kingdom purposes, you will find greater fulfillment, joy, and impact in everything you do.

Reflect

Write a prayer asking God to help you see your work as a reflection of His glory. Commit to seeking His kingdom first in all you do, trusting that He will provide for your needs and guide you in fulfilling your purpose.

Next Steps

- Identify three goals for transforming your work into a vocation that reflects God's glory.
- Set a monthly reminder to revisit this workbook to track your progress and adjust your goals as needed.

Prayer

Lord, help me to see my work as a divine calling, not just a job. Help me align my labor with Your kingdom purposes, and let everything I do reflect Your glory and bring honor to Your name. Amen.

CHAPTER 6

THE RESTORATION OF PURPOSEFUL WORK

The restoration of purposeful work comes when it is done for God's glory. This worship transcends mere self-serving pursuits and aligns our work with eternal purposes. Through faith, we can discover work that honors God as opposed to jobs that keep us from co-creating with God. The notion of worship and service is at the heart of our work and benefits us and others.

This chapter is designed to help you explore a higher understanding of work and worship and make a lasting impact for God's kingdom. We must explore the pitfalls of self-worship and the eternal value of dedicating one's work to God.

Rediscovering Purpose in Work

Work was never meant to be burdensome or solely self-serving. In God's original design, work is a co-creative activity done in partnership with Him. Our challenge today is to reclaim the meaning and purpose in our labor, understanding that it is a form of worship that brings glory to God.

Work as Worship

Work is not just a means of survival; it is an act of worship when done with the right intention. When we dedicate our work to God, it transcends earthly significance and becomes an expression of service to Him.

Reflect

1. How is your work co-creative with God?

2. What adjustments can you make to better align your work with God's purpose?

Worship Through Work Journal

For the next five days, keep a journal of your daily tasks at work. Before starting each task, offer it to God in prayer, asking Him to bless your work. At the end of the week, reflect on how this practice impacted your attitude and experience.

Avoiding the Pitfalls of Self-Worship

When we focus on working for ourselves—whether for wealth, status, or personal gain—we fall into the trap of self-worship. This mindset leads to emptiness and dissatisfaction, as seen in King Solomon's reflections on the futility of work done for selfish purposes.

Reflect

1. Are there areas in your life where you are working more for personal gain than for God's glory?

2. Why do you view these areas more for personal gain?

3. How can you shift your motivation to prioritize God's eternal purposes in your work?

Realigning Goals

Write down three goals you currently have in your professional life. Next to each goal, identify whether it is primarily self-serving or aligned with God's kingdom. For each self-serving goal, write down one way you can shift your focus to make it a kingdom-centered goal.

Trusting God With Your Resources

Just as Jesus taught in the parable of the talents, God calls us to trust Him with what we have, using our gifts and resources to serve His purposes. A scarcity mindset, or a fear of losing what we have, can keep us from fully stepping into our God-given calling.

Reflect

1. What talents or resources has God given you that you've been hesitant to use fully for His glory?

2. How can you release control and trust God to multiply your efforts?

Talents Inventory

Make a list of your skills, talents, and resources. For each one, write down how you are currently using it. Then, write down one new way you can use each one to serve God and others in a greater capacity.

Overcoming Fear of God's Plan for Our Work

Many people live beholden to a job they despise, or they have jobs that do not worship God. Discovering God's plan for work involves embracing the truth that work is part of God's original design for humanity given to us before the Fall as a means to reflect His image. Understanding work as a calling, rather than a burden empowers us to approach it with a sense of significance. By aligning our work with God's greater purpose, we can overcome fear and confidently engage in meaningful, impactful work that honors Him.

Reflect

1. How does viewing work as part of God's original design shift your perspective on your daily tasks and responsibilities?

2. In what ways can you begin to align your work with God's greater purpose, and how can this help you overcome any fear or discouragement you may feel in your work?

Work as a Calling

Write down one task or responsibility you feel is a burden in your work. Reflect on how this task could be seen as part of God's greater purpose for you. Reframe this task as an opportunity to reflect His creativity and purpose, and write down a plan to approach it with a renewed mindset.

Co-Creating With God

We are co-creators with God, participating in His plan for the world through our work. Whether it's through innovation, leadership, or service, our work is an opportunity to reflect God's creative power.

Reflect

1. How would your work look different if you viewed it as a collaboration with God?

2. In what ways can you bring creativity and excellence into your daily tasks as a reflection of God's nature?

Co-Creator Project

Choose one task or project at work where you can intentionally collaborate with God. This could involve seeking His guidance in decision-making, approaching a challenge with creativity, or serving others with excellence. Write down how this collaboration transforms your approach and outcome.

Performance, Image, and Exposure (PIE)

In your work, God calls you to perform with excellence, bear His image, and be exposed to the world as a representative of His kingdom. This principle is reflected in the stories of Joseph, Daniel, and David.

Reflect

1. Review the stories of Joseph, Daniel, and David. Do you see similarities with your life? How?

2. Using the stories of Joseph, Daniel, and David as examples, how can you incorporate PIE into your work?

PIE Evaluation

Using the PIE model (Performance, Image, Exposure), evaluate your current role in the workplace. List one way you can improve your performance, one way you can better reflect God's image, and one step you can take to increase your exposure or influence for God's kingdom.

Set Apart for God's Use

Paul calls believers to present their bodies as living sacrifices, set apart for God's use. This means dedicating our physical, mental, and emotional efforts to God's work, consecrating all we do as an act of worship.

Reflect

1. What areas of your work life need to be set apart for God's use?

2. How can you consecrate your time, energy, and resources to serve God more fully?

Consecration Prayer

Spend time in prayer, asking God to reveal any areas of your work that need to be set apart for His use. Write a prayer of dedication, offering these areas to God and asking for His guidance in using them for His glory.

Restoring the Joy of Work

When our work is aligned with God's will, it brings fulfillment and joy. Solomon reminds us that when we work for God's glory, we can enjoy the fruits of our labor as a gift from Him.

Reflect

1. Do you find joy in your current work? If not, what needs to change to bring about that joy?

2. How can you practice gratitude for the work God has given you?

Gratitude List

Write down five things you are grateful for in your work, no matter how small. Add to this list each day, and reflect on how practicing gratitude transforms your attitude toward your labor.

Living With Eternal Purpose

Work done solely for personal gain is fleeting and ultimately meaningless. However, when we work with eternity in mind, we contribute to God's kingdom and leave a lasting impact.

Reflect

1. How does your work contribute to God's eternal purposes?

2. What legacy do you want to leave through your work?

Eternal Legacy Plan

Write down one long-term goal for your work that has eternal significance. Create a plan for how you can take practical steps toward achieving this goal.

Building God's Kingdom Through Work

When we prioritize building God's kingdom through our work, everything else falls into place. This means using our gifts, resources, and opportunities to advance His purposes on earth.

Reflect

1. What does it mean to seek God's kingdom first in your work?

2. How can you intentionally build God's kingdom in your workplace or community?

Kingdom-Building Action Plan

Write down three specific actions you can take in the next month to build God's kingdom through your work. This could include serving others, sharing your faith, or improving your work environment to reflect kingdom values.

Figuring Out Your Divine Purpose

Work is more than just a job; it is a divine calling that allows us to worship, serve, and co-create with God. By aligning our work with God's eternal purposes, we can find true fulfillment and leave a lasting impact for His kingdom.

Next Steps

- Set three specific goals for aligning your work with God's kingdom purposes.
- Revisit this workbook regularly to track your progress and reflect on how God is shaping your work for His glory.

Prayer

Lord, I dedicate my work to You. Help me to align my labor with Your kingdom purposes and to serve You with joy and gratitude. Empower me to perform with excellence, bear Your image, and be exposed to the world for Your glory. Amen.

CHAPTER 7

THE POWER TO GET WEALTH

Our work in the marketplace is not just commercial. Instead, it is an opportunity to extend God's kingdom on earth as it is in heaven. Whatever God has purposed us to do on earth, He is more than able to provide the necessary resources to accomplish His will and purpose.

This chapter will help you explore the biblical perspective on wealth, work, and marketplace ministry. You will learn how to align your efforts in the marketplace with God's plan for prosperity and purpose.

Wealth as a Tool for God's Kingdom

God's desires His people to use their skills, creativity, and resources to fulfill His purposes in the marketplace. Wealth is not merely about financial prosperity but also the power to influence, solve problems, and serve others.

Understanding the Purpose of Wealth

Wealth in God's kingdom is a tool for advancing His purposes. It enables us to provide for ourselves, meet the needs of others, and extend God's kingdom on earth.

Reflect

1. How do you currently view wealth—primarily as a personal gain or a tool for service and influence? Why?

2. In what ways can you align your understanding of wealth with God's eternal purposes?

Wealth Purpose Chart

Create a chart to explore how the wealth (material and nonmaterial) that you currently have can be used to serve others and fulfill God's kingdom purposes. Identify areas where you could be more intentional in using your resources for God's work.

Co-Creating With God in the Marketplace

God has designed us to be co-creators with Him, using our talents, skills, and resources to solve problems and innovate. The marketplace is not merely a secular space but a mission field where God's principles can be applied.

Reflect

1. How do you see yourself as a co-creator with God in your current role in the marketplace?

2. What specific problems can you help solve in your workplace or community that reflect God's creativity and love?

Problem-Solving Project
Identify one challenge you feel called to address in your workplace or community. Write a plan for creatively solving this problem using the talents and resources God has given you. Set goals and record your progress over the next month.

Faith Overcoming Fear

Fear often holds us back from realizing our full potential in the marketplace. God has given us the power to overcome fear and trust His provision as we seek to fulfill His purposes.

Reflect
1. What fears hold you back from new opportunities or taking risks?

2. How can you use faith to overcome these fears and trust God's provision?

Faith in Action
Choose one fear that is preventing you from moving forward. Write down a practical step of faith that you will take this week to overcome that fear. Record your results and reflect on how faith helped you move forward.

Generosity as a Key to Prosperity

God calls us to be generous with the resources He provides. Prosperity includes sharing with others and contributing to the common good.

Reflect

1. How can generosity transform your approach to wealth and success?

2. How can you practice generosity with your current resources, no matter how limited they may seem?

Generosity Plan

Create a generosity plan for the next month. Identify ways you can share your time, resources, or skills with others. Make it a priority to practice generosity regularly and track the impact it has on your heart and your relationships.

Overcoming a Safety Mindset

We are hardwired for safety, but God calls us to step out of our comfort zones and trust Him with the unknown. This requires overcoming the fear of scarcity and embracing the abundance God promises.

Reflect

1. Where in your life are you stuck in a safety mindset that is preventing growth?

2. What would it look like to trust God with your resources and step into abundance?

Abundance Mindset Challenge

For one week, practice a mindset of abundance rather than scarcity. Each day, identify one area where you can release control and trust God's provision. Reflect on and journal about how this mindset shift affects your outlook and decisions.

The Power of Words

The words we speak shape our reality. When we declare God's promises and align our speech with His will, we open the door for His power to work in our lives.

Reflect

1. How do your words reflect your beliefs about wealth, work, and God's provision?

2. What declarations can you make to align your words with God's promises?

Positive Declarations

Write five positive declarations based on God's Word that you will speak over your life and work each day for the next week. At the end of the week, reflect on how these declarations have influenced your mindset and actions.

Stewardship of Resources

God calls us to be wise stewards of the resources He provides, using them to fulfill His purposes and to bless others. Stewardship requires careful planning, intentional giving, and responsible management.

Reflect

1. How are you currently stewarding the resources God has given you?

2. What changes can you make to be a better steward and align your actions with God's will?

Stewardship Assessment

Conduct a personal or business stewardship assessment. Identify areas where you are managing resources well and areas where improvement is needed. Develop a plan to make better use of what God has entrusted to you.

The Purpose of Wealth in Serving Others

Wealth is not an end in itself. Its true purpose is to serve others and to further God's kingdom on earth. By using wealth to solve problems and meet the needs of others, we fulfill God's purpose for prosperity.

Reflect

1. How does your current approach to wealth and success reflect God's call to serve others?

2. How can you use your resources to solve problems and improve the lives of those around you?

Service Project Plan

Develop a service project that allows you to use your wealth or talents to meet needs in your community or workplace. This could be anything from organizing a charity drive to offering free professional services. Set a timeline and actionable steps to complete this project.

Walking in Your Divine Calling

God has a specific calling for each of us in the marketplace. When we align our work with His calling, we find greater purpose and fulfillment.

Reflect

1. Are you walking in alignment with God's calling for your life?

2. How can you further align your work or business with God's purpose?

Calling Clarification

Spend time in prayer, asking God to reveal or confirm His calling for your life. Write down what you feel He is calling you to do, and create an action plan to begin walking in that calling with greater intentionality.

Leaving a Legacy of Impact

True wealth is about leaving a legacy of faith, generosity, and impact. This goes beyond financial inheritance to include the values and principles we pass down to future generations.

Reflect

1. What kind of legacy do you want to leave for your family, community, or industry?

2. How can you begin building that legacy today?

Legacy Plan

Write a legacy plan that outlines the values, principles, and resources you want to pass down to the next generation. Include specific actions you can take now to ensure your legacy aligns with God's will.

Walking in the Power to Get Wealth

God's plan for wealth goes beyond personal gain; it involves using the resources He provides to solve problems, bless others, and expand His kingdom. As you walk in alignment with God's purposes, you will experience the fulfillment that comes from being a faithful steward and co-creator with Him.

Prayer Exercise

Write a prayer asking God to help you walk in the power to get wealth, trusting Him with your resources and using them to serve His kingdom. Commit to living with generosity, purpose, and faith as you navigate the marketplace.

Next Steps

- Identify three specific goals related to wealth and stewardship that you will pursue in the next three months.
- Revisit this workbook regularly to reflect on your progress and seek God's guidance in your journey.

Prayer

Lord, thank You for the power You have given me to create wealth. Help me to use this power to serve others, fulfill Your purposes, and expand Your kingdom. May everything I do bring glory to Your name and reflect Your love and generosity to the world. Amen.

CHAPTER 8

THE COVENANT OF PROSPERITY

Knowing God's excellent track record with covenants stretching back to the Old Testament, we can be confident that God is a God who keeps His Word. God has promised to take care of us, and we can rest in His faithfulness as we continue to work and represent God in the marketplace.

This chapter explores the biblical concept of prosperity as part of God's covenant with His people. You will gain a deeper understanding of how God's promises of prosperity can be activated in your life, especially as you serve in the marketplace.

The Foundation of Covenant Prosperity

God's covenant of prosperity is not limited to financial success but includes spiritual, emotional, and relational wealth. This covenant reminds us that God empowers His people to succeed, not for selfish gain but to fulfill His purpose and extend His kingdom.

The covenant God made with His people throughout the Bible demonstrates His unwavering commitment to their well-being and success. From the Noahic covenant of preservation to the Christ covenant of grace, God's promises are designed to bless His people and enable them to be a blessing to others.

Reflect
1. How do you understand prosperity within the context of God's covenant?

2. In what ways has God's covenantal promise of prosperity already been fulfilled in your life?

Covenant Reflection

Reflect on the biblical covenants mentioned in the text (Noahic, Abrahamic, Mosaic, and Christ covenant). Write a brief paragraph about each covenant and how it demonstrates God's commitment to His people. Then reflect on how the covenant of prosperity applies to your life today.

God's Provision and Prosperity

God promises to provide for His people in every aspect of life. Whether through material resources, wisdom, or divine opportunities, God's provision is always aligned with His purpose for us.

Reflect

1. What does God's provision look like in your life?

2. How can you trust God more fully to provide for your material and spiritual needs?

Provision Inventory

List of the ways God has provided for you in the past month. This could include financial resources, relationships, opportunities, or spiritual blessings. Reflect on how God's provision has enabled you to fulfill His purposes in your life and work.

Overcoming Fear and Embracing Faith

Fear often prevents us from embracing God's promise of prosperity. However, when we align our actions with faith, trusting in God's plan, we step into His provision and experience the fullness of His blessings.

Reflect

1. What fears are holding you back from fully embracing God's promises?

2. How can you strengthen your faith to overcome these fears?

Fear to Faith Exercise

Write down three fears you have about your work, finances, or future. Next to each fear, write a Scripture that addresses it and a corresponding faith-based action you can take this week to move beyond fear. At the end of the week, reflect on how taking these steps has strengthened your trust in God.

The Power to Get Wealth

God gives His people the power and ability to create wealth, not for selfish gain but to fulfill His covenant. Wealth is a tool for serving others, solving problems, and advancing God's kingdom.

Reflect

1. How do you view your ability to create wealth in the context of God's purpose for your life?

2. How can you use your resources to benefit others and extend God's kingdom?

Wealth Creation Plan

Identify one area where you feel God is calling you to create wealth. Write down a plan that includes practical steps to use this wealth to serve others and contribute to God's purposes. Set a timeline for each step and track your progress.

Stewardship and Generosity

As part of God's covenant, we are called to be good stewards of the resources He provides. Stewardship involves using wealth wisely and generously, ensuring that it benefits us and others.

Reflect

1. How well are you stewarding the resources God has given you?

2. In what areas of your life can you practice greater generosity?

Generosity Challenge

Choose one area where you can practice generosity this week. Set a goal for how you will give generously, and at the end of the week, reflect on how this act of generosity impacted you and the recipient.

Work: God's Divine Plan for Kingdom Prosperity
Your work is God's plan to bring kingdom prosperity to your life. When you align your work with God's purposes, you unlock the potential to prosper in ways that serve others and glorify Him.

Reflect
1. How does your work align with God's kingdom purposes?

2. What steps can you take to ensure your work is fulfilling God's plan?

Kingdom Purpose Assessment
Evaluate your current job or business, and identify how it contributes to God's kingdom. Write down three specific ways you can enhance this contribution, whether through serving others, solving problems, or demonstrating Christ-like leadership in your field.

Fear of Not Having Enough

Many people struggle with a scarcity mindset, believing there is not enough to go around. However, God's covenant promises abundance, and we are called to trust Him for provision and to live with an abundance mentality.

Reflect

1. Where do you struggle with a scarcity mindset?

2. How can you shift to an abundance mentality based on God's promises?

Abundance Declaration

Each morning for the next week, declare an abundance affirmation over your life such as: "God is my provider, and He has more than enough to meet my needs." Write down any changes you notice in your mindset and behavior as a result of this practice.

Covenant Faithfulness and Timing

God is faithful to fulfill His promises, but His timing may not always align with our expectations. Learning to trust God's timing is essential for experiencing the fullness of His covenant blessings.

Reflect

1. How have you experienced delays in seeing God's promises fulfilled?

2. How can you practice patience and faithfulness while waiting on God's timing?

Patience in Action

Identify one area where you feel you are waiting on God's timing. Write down a prayer asking for patience and trust during this waiting period. Each day, reflect on how God's timing has been perfect in the past and how you can trust Him for the future.

Words of Affirmation and Power

The words we speak carry power. Speaking words of affirmation that align with God's promises helps us activate those promises in our lives and overcome challenges with faith.

Reflect

1. How do your words reflect your faith in God's promises?

2. What changes can you make to speak life over your work, finances, and relationships?

Daily Affirmations

Create a list of ten affirmations based on God's Word. Speak these affirmations aloud each morning for the next week, and reflect on how they influence your mindset and actions.

Living in Covenant Prosperity

Living in the covenant of prosperity means trusting God to fulfill His promises and using the resources He provides to bless others. Prosperity is about wealth and living a life of purpose, service, and faith.

Reflect

1. How can you fully embrace God's covenant of prosperity?

2. How can you use your prosperity to bless others and further God's kingdom?

Next Steps

- Set three specific goals for aligning your life with God's covenant promises.
- Revisit this workbook regularly to reflect on your progress and seek God's guidance in your journey.

Prayer

Lord, thank You for Your covenant of prosperity. Help me trust You and use your resources to serve others and bring glory to Your name. Amen.